Dear Parents:

Congratulations! Your child is taking the first steps on an exciting journey. The destination? Independent reading!

STEP INTO READING® will help your child get there. The program offers five steps to reading success. Each step includes fun stories and colorful art or photographs. In addition to original fiction and books with favorite characters, there are Step into Reading Non-Fiction Readers, Phonics Readers and Boxed Sets, Sticker Readers, and Comic Readers—a complete literacy program with something to interest every child.

Learning to Read, Step by Step!

Ready to Read   **Preschool–Kindergarten**
• big type and easy words • rhyme and rhythm • picture clues
For children who know the alphabet and are eager to begin reading.

Reading with Help   **Preschool–Grade 1**
• basic vocabulary • short sentences • simple stories
For children who recognize familiar words and sound out new words with help.

Reading on Your Own   **Grades 1–3**
• engaging characters • easy-to-follow plots • popular topics
For children who are ready to read on their own.

Reading Paragraphs   **Grades 2–3**
• challenging vocabulary • short paragraphs • exciting stories
For newly independent readers who read simple sentences with confidence.

Ready for Chapters   **Grades 2–4**
• chapters • longer paragraphs • full-color art
For children who want to take the plunge into chapter books but still like colorful pictures.

STEP INTO READING® is designed to give every child a successful reading experience. The grade levels are only guides; children will progress through the steps at their own speed, developing confidence in their reading.

Remember, a lifetime love of reading starts with a single step!

To Wilson, Emma, and all my other
feline friends, past and present.
—S. F.

Copyright © 2021 DC Comics.
BATMAN and all related characters and elements
© & ™ DC Comics. WB SHIELD: ™ & © Warner Bros. Entertainment Inc.
(s21)

Published in the United States by Random House Children's Books, a division of Penguin Random House LLC, 1745 Broadway, New York, NY 10019, and in Canada by Penguin Random House Canada Limited, Toronto.

Step into Reading, Random House, and the Random House colophon are registered trademarks of Penguin Random House LLC.

Visit us on the Web!
StepIntoReading.com
rhcbooks.com

Educators and librarians, for a variety of teaching tools, visit us at RHTeachersLibrarians.com

ISBN 978-0-593-30436-5 (trade) — ISBN 978-0-593-30437-2 (lib. bdg.)
ISBN 978-0-593-30438-9 (ebook)

Printed in the United States of America   10 9 8 7 6 5 4 3 2 1

BATMAN™

COPYCAT!

by Steve Foxe

illustrated by Fabio Laguna and Marco Lesko

Batman created by Bob Kane with Bill Finger

Random House 🏠 New York

Batman swung across
the Gotham City rooftops.
He was almost done
with his patrol
when he spotted a robbery!

Batman swooped over
to a broken window.

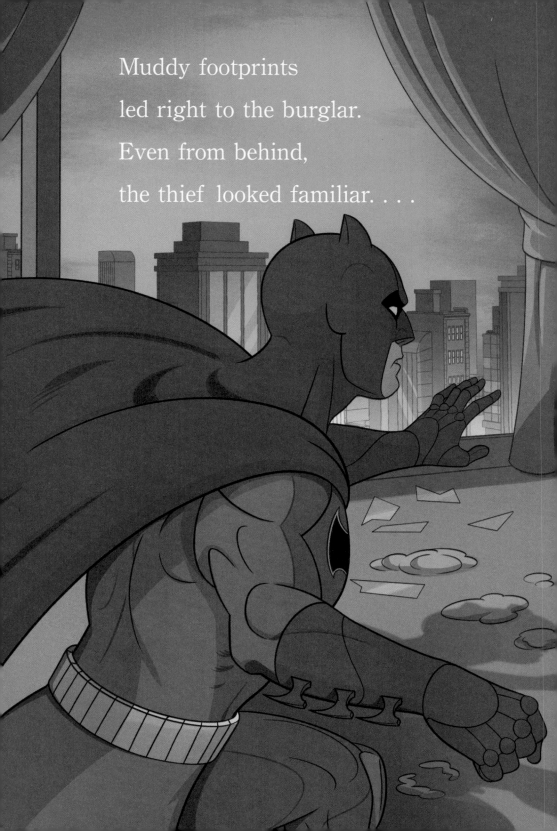

Muddy footprints
led right to the burglar.
Even from behind,
the thief looked familiar. . . .

"Catwoman!" Batman said.

The thief looked over her shoulder
and snarled.

She continued to steal jewels
from a vault.

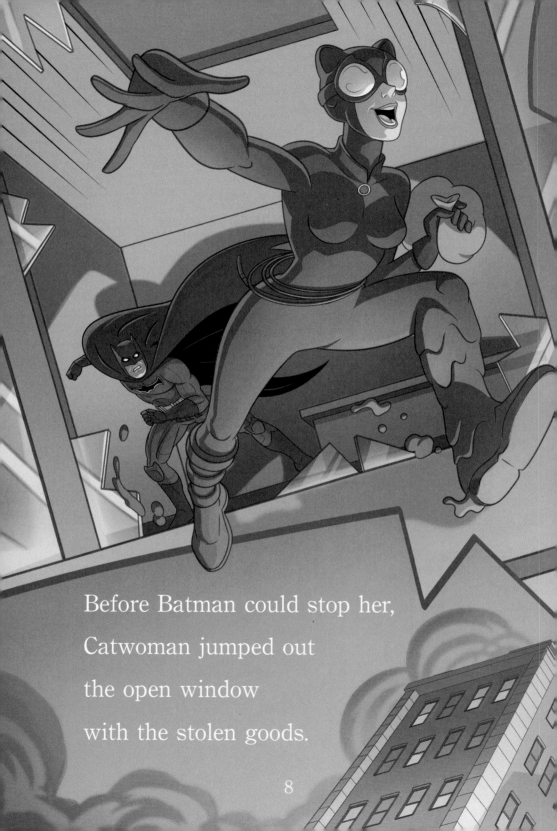

Before Batman could stop her,
Catwoman jumped out
the open window
with the stolen goods.

WHOOSH!

Batman followed the silent thief.
He thought about the footprints,
and how Catwoman was never
that sloppy.

Batman landed on a nearby roof.

He couldn't believe his eyes.

Catwoman was about to fight . . .

Catwoman!

"Help me catch this copycat!"
the real Catwoman said.
But the thief jumped off the roof
before Batman could grab her!

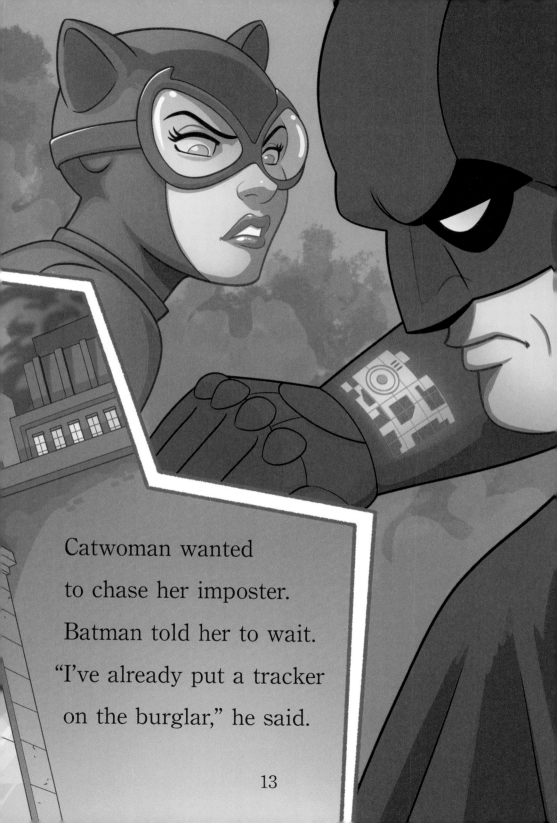

Catwoman wanted
to chase her imposter.
Batman told her to wait.
"I've already put a tracker
on the burglar," he said.

13

Batman used a remote control
to call the Batplane
so he and Catwoman
could follow the tracking signal.

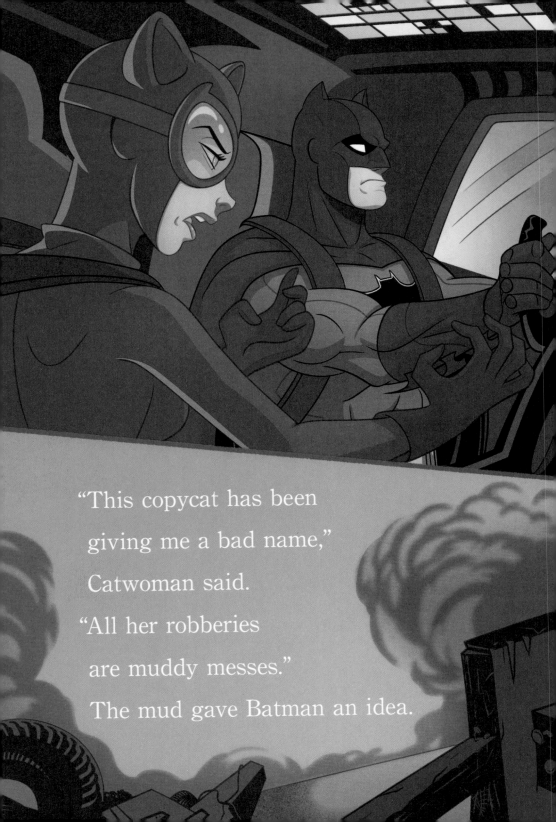

"This copycat has been
giving me a bad name,"
Catwoman said.
"All her robberies
are muddy messes."
The mud gave Batman an idea.

The tracking signal stopped
at an old warehouse.
Batman landed the Batplane.
He and Catwoman
quietly slipped into
the dark building.

They found the thief right away.

Batman pulled out his Batarang.

He threw it
at a sprinkler.

Water went everywhere.
The fake Catwoman
got soaked!

The copycat melted away, revealing the villain Clayface! "How did you know it was me?" Clayface asked.

"Your muddy footprints
gave you away,"
Batman explained.

"I wanted to pin these robberies
on Catwoman!"
Clayface shouted.
The muddy villain
formed his arm
into a giant hammer.

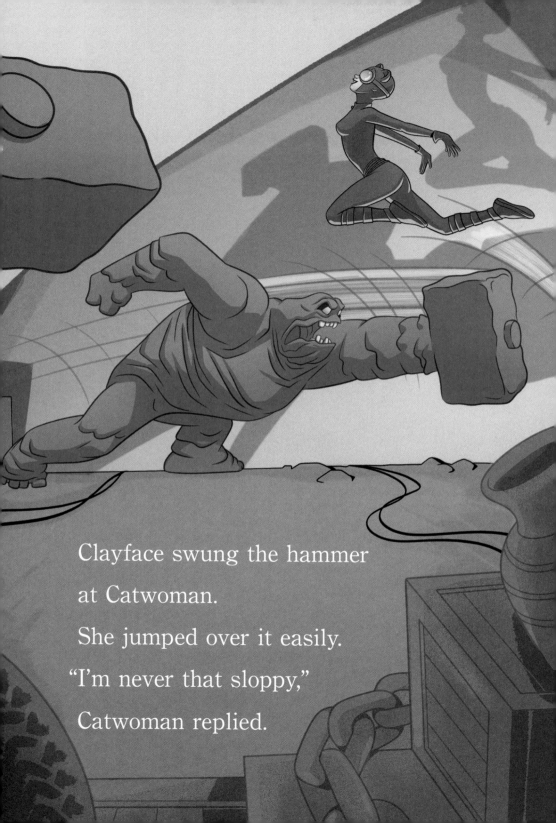

Clayface swung the hammer
at Catwoman.
She jumped over it easily.
"I'm never that sloppy,"
Catwoman replied.

Clayface formed his other arm
into a spiked ball.
Batman braced himself
to dodge an attack.

Clayface swung his arm—
SMASH!

The wall behind Batman
and Catwoman broke apart
and fell on them!

Batman was prepared.
He used his gauntlets
to block the falling rubble.

While no one was looking,
Clayface tried to transform
into Batman.
He thought a new disguise
would help him escape
Catwoman's revenge.

Catwoman spotted Clayface
before he could finish!
She used her whip to grab him.
"Sorry, Clayface,"
she said.
"Your acting days are over."

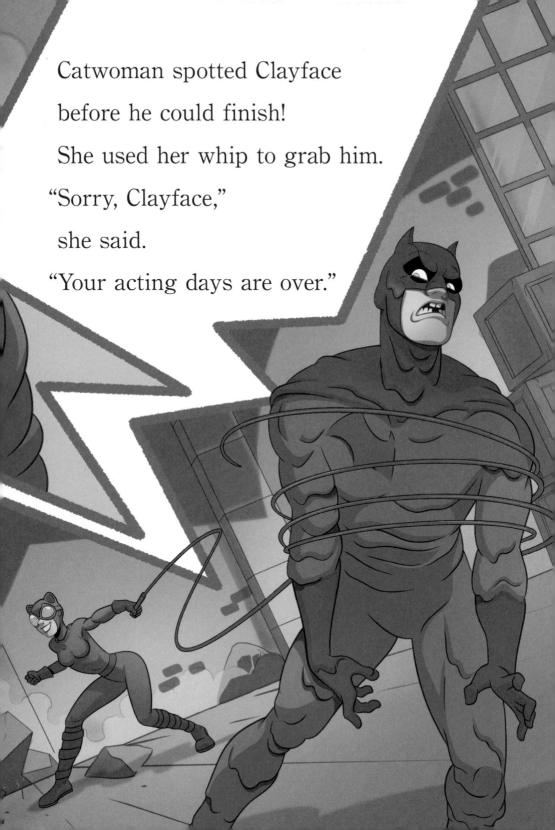

Clayface tried to melt
out of Catwoman's grip,
but Batman quickly grabbed
a handful of ice pellets
from his Utility Belt
and threw them at the villain.

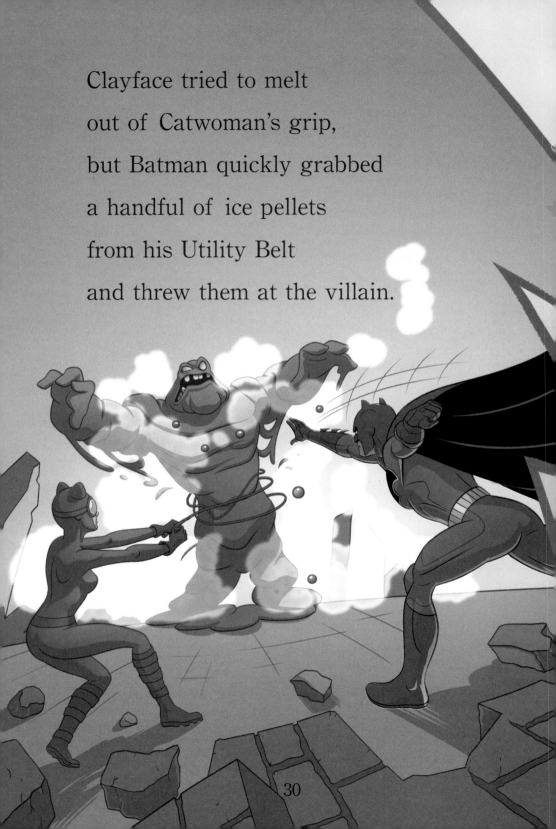

Clayface roared
as the gas
froze him solid!
Within seconds,
the villain became
a statue of ice.

Catwoman looked at
the stolen jewels.
"Don't worry," Batman said.
"I'll make sure these get back
to where they belong."